The Magic of Princess Patsy

Written by Sharon Kusterer
Illustrated by Liz Mallia

The Magic of Princess Patsy

by Sharon Kusterer

Copyright ©2021 by Sharon Kusterer

Editor: Suzanne Fregly

Illustrator: Liz Mallia

Photography: Sharon Kusterer

Book Design: Herb Neu

ISBN 978-0-9963837-3-8

SIMPSON POINT PRESS

Published by Simpson Point Press • P.O. Box 205 • Grant, AL 35747 USA

www.simpsonpointpress.com

Foreword

Patsy, the Pekinese, came into my life in 2017. An orphan myself, I have always held a special place in my heart for homeless and lost animals. My daughter, Jackie, a veterinary student in Budapest, Hungary, first told me about Patsy when a Hungarian rescue group called the Foundation of Animal Protection in Fuezesabony, or FAPF, found her abandoned and near death under a snow-covered bush in Budapest. After FAPF ensured that her health was stabilized, it put her up for adoption. Jackie, a volunteer with the organization and Patsy's foster mom, told me I would love her gentle spirit and joyful personality, but my husband and I already had two dogs, so I declined her offer.

When two other potential adoptions fell through, Jackie decided to adopt Patsy. A year later, Jackie returned to Germany to finish her studies. Patsy spent a lot of time with my husband and me, and we noticed right away that she is a very special dog who brings smiles to everyone she meets. Her cute waddle and her vampire smile win many hearts, and she captures the attention of many. She has an innate nurturing spirit that seems to be present with every animal, cats and dogs alike. Patsy is also a best friend to Jackie, and they share a very special connection.

Not too long ago, a vet visit and ultrasound showed that Patsy has an enlarged heart and a degenerative heart condition. To us, it is no surprise that she has an enlarged heart, because she spreads joy and love wherever she goes. The vet gave her medicine and recently told Jackie that Patsy's condition is worsening, and she doesn't have long to live. I always wanted to write a children's book about Patsy, but hearing this news inspired me to get it done in her honor, and as a gift for Jackie.

I hope this book and its magic will inspire readers not only to consider adopting a rescue dog, but also to know that losing those we love, whether family members, friends or pets, doesn't mean that because they have left the physical world, they are gone forever. The most beautiful thing to discover is that they can live on in our hearts, and if we tune in, we can experience their love, just as we did when they were here. Knowing they never leave us can empower us to heal and embrace the loving energy we need to get through difficult times.

Sharon Kusterer

The Magic of Princess Patsy

My name is *Princess Patsy.* I'm a 10-year-old Pekinese rescue dog from Budapest, and I have a degenerative heart disease. That means that my heart could stop beating at any time, and I have to take medicine and go to the vet quite often. The vet told my owner that my heart condition will get worse, and one day, my heart will stop beating forever.

Many other dogs like me—and other breeds that come in all shapes and sizes—also have heart and other medical conditions. You can find them all over the world.

My story begins on the day something happened to me that changed everything. My owner decided I was too sick. He couldn't keep me anymore, so he dropped me off at a gas station near the highway. He didn't want to do that, but he just couldn't afford the vet's bills to take care of me. It was winter and freezing cold when he left me there. I didn't know what to do, so I found a snow-covered bush to sleep under and hoped he'd change his mind and come back to get me.

Over the next several days, I was so cold, tired and hungry, and my heart ached that my owner hadn't realized he'd made a mistake and come back to fetch me. Under the bush, I'd occasionally gather all my strength, then stumble over to the gas station. The nice people there would sometimes feed me a hot dog and scraps and send me on my way again. I was very scared and felt so alone.

Sometimes, to help myself feel better, I'd imagine I was a princess in a beautiful castle. There I'd be warm, have a full belly and live in a kingdom where everyone loved me.

A few days later, as I became weaker and weaker, FAPF found me. My heart was beating very slowly, and I couldn't breathe well anymore. I then finally realized my owner was never coming back.

FAPF's rescue team took me to a toasty-warm, heated house and

wrapped me in a soft blanket. They gave me real dog food and some toys fit for a princess, and I slept a lot. Slowly, I regained my strength, and I was so happy! My princess dream had come true!

Within a few days, I felt better and stronger. Soon a veterinary student named Jackie, who was originally from Germany, adopted me. We eventually moved there together, and I continued to get healthier. I also had Leberwurst (liver pate) for the first time. Taking my heart medicine with Leberwurst was the best!

While living with Jackie, my royal kingdom grew. So many people loved me! I often stayed with Jackie's parents when she had to go away, and I met so many new friends from all over the world.

In my new home, I felt safe and was sure I'd be completely healthy again. I had so much fun spending time with Jackie. She took me everywhere, and I met so many new dog friends. I even had two other FAPF rescue animals—cats named Luna and Art—to cuddle up with for a while.

I loved meeting all my new friends, but my heart ached so badly when they left. I never knew whether I'd see them again, just as I felt when my former owner left me at the gas station. I wanted them to stay with me in my great new kingdom, so we could all be together. This became my biggest wish.

Then one morning, something very strange happened. I woke up, and my heart felt much bigger in my chest, my two canine teeth were sharp and pointy, and I looked like a vampire when I smiled. My paws were webbed, and tufts of hair sprouted at the tips of my toes, so I looked like a duck and waddled when I walked.

To my surprise, people somehow noticed me even more and said how cute I was. It didn't matter that I was different from other dogs. I was still Princess Patsy inside. Strangers kept smiling when they saw me. I seemed to bring joy to everyone I met, with my vampire teeth and duck waddle. Even the grumpiest old people would turn around and smile as they saw me passing. My big heart was beating stronger than ever!

Of course, it took time for this princess to get used to her new look. Can you imagine waking up with vampire teeth and webbed feet?

Soon it became fun, though, and each day I smiled with my vampire teeth and waddled on my morning and afternoon walks. Everyone continued to notice and smile back at me. It made me wonder whether their hearts also got bigger during their short meetings with me, the princess with vampire teeth and webbed paws.

While walking in the park with Jackie one day, I decided to create a princess poopy dance. I turned my waddle into a quick little dance, as I excitedly searched for the perfect spot to poop.

Jackie often worried that I'd get lost during the poopy dance, because I got so excited, danced and ran so fast, I'd forget where I was.

After creating the poopy dance, I realized I had magic powers, just like a real princess. During a walk, I'd sometimes stop and consider what to do next to bring people joy. A few times, I walked up to the front door of a nearby house, simply wanting to introduce myself and spread more smiles.

I could go anywhere with my magic powers. Another fun thing I liked to do was go up to cars whose trunks people were loading and unloading. With my magic powers, I could jump onto the front seat and go on a ride with anyone I chose. Riding in the car was one of my favorite things to do in the whole world!

When I finished contemplating or visiting a new place, I'd excitedly run back to Jackie, who stood waiting nearby, happy to see me.

It seemed only natural to use my special magic powers to bring all the people and animals I loved to live together in my perfect kingdom. Isn't that the way life should be? If I could bring joy and smiles, why couldn't I also bring all the people I loved to live together with me?

I smiled a bigger vampire-teeth smile, waddled around with my webbed paws and performed my poopy dance perfectly. I imagined that everyone was together, and I sent out love from my big heart, doing my very best to get their attention.   However, the people I loved continued to come and go and change directions all the time, without any thought. I kept trying, but it just didn't work out the way I'd hoped. I felt so sad. No one was listening or paying attention, or perhaps they didn't even want to be part of my kingdom.

I loved Jackie more than dog biscuits themselves, but I still dreamed of keeping my princess pack together. Over time, I realized that the friends I loved never really left me, even though they drove away, walked away or left Jackie's house. My heart was so big— and grew even bigger— when I discovered I could spread my love energy to fill their hearts at any time and place in the world, without actually being there!

Knowing this, I felt my big heart grow bigger than ever before. I connected to so many people with my magic powers, and I brought laughter and smiles to even the saddest people, everywhere I went. I liked being different, a big-hearted princess with vampire teeth and webbed paws. I loved my poopy dance, too. All these qualities make me unique and are part of the special princess I am.

I still have a degenerative heart disease, but I have learned to love being me and appreciate every moment I have to grow my heart even bigger and stronger. It's the best feeling ever to have a big heart and magic princess powers that can spread happiness and love wherever I go. This is my mission and keeps my heart beating strongly. I still have a big job to do!

So to all you children who have a pet with a disease like mine, or whose pet has already gone to that magical kingdom in the sky, please know that we love you and will always be with you at heart during good times and bad, just as we know how much love you have—and will always have—for us. I promise that we'll meet again.

With love, always, from my big heart to yours,

Princess Patsy

Acknowledgments

I would like to extend my appreciation and a big thank-you to *Zsanett Molnár* and the *Foundation of Animal Protection in Fuezesabony (FAPF),* for their tireless dedication and commitment to rescuing and re-housing animals; to *Liz Mallia,* Patsy's friend from Budapest, for the beautiful illustrations; to *Suzanne Fregly,* for her editing and ongoing support; to my husband, *Wolfram Kusterer,* whose love and never-ending patience have helped me to heal and reach new heights I never expected; to my son, *Kevin,* for all of his love and encouragement; to my publisher, *Herb Neu,* for his shared love of animals and his expertise in creating this book; and to my daughter, *Jackie,* for the great care she has given Patsy, allowing us to fully experience the love, joy and healing that Patsy's real-life magic has brought into the world.

About the Author

Originally from California, Sharon Kusterer lives with her husband in southern Germany, has two adult children and has a 13-year-old Maltese called Nicky. She is a communication empowerment coach, speaker and college lecturer.

"Animals are truly magical and can help us heal in ways no human can."

Patsy, on the right, with her best friend, Nicky.

To see more fun photos of Princess Patsy and her friends, please go to www.princesspatsy.com.

Made in the USA
Monee, IL
07 July 2026